BMX BLITZ

FOLLOWED BY:

D1353037

KID$

ULTIMATE BMX RACE COURSE AWAITS TOP TEEN BIKERS

LUKE LAWLESS

STATS:
AGE: 14
COLOURS: GREEN/WHITE

BIO: Luke Lawless is a top-ranked teen BMX biker who has travelled a long way to compete in the BMX-Blitz. The super-secret, brand-new race course has been kept under wraps during its development, so no one knows exactly what to expect. But one thing's for certain – this will be the wildest ride Luke Lawless has ever experienced.

HOUSTON MORIKAMI

AGE: 15
COLOURS: PINK/WHITE

BIO: Houston is the only female competitor in the BMX-Blitz – but she doesn't care. Houston's been beating boys on the race course since she first put foot to pedal.

PETER HILDEBRAND

AGE: 14   **COLOURS:** BLACK/SILVER
BIO: Peter is the son of a wealthy CEO and has all the best biking gear. On the race course, Peter is as ruthless as his businessman father.

PETER

DENNY LAWLESS

AGE: 42
BIO: Luke Lawless's father, Denny, is a famous NASCAR driver who isn't all that interested in BMX racing.

DENNY

THE MORIKAMIS

FIRST NAMES: HUAN AND KAZU
BIO: The Morikamis do not approve of their daughter competing in BMX races. They would rather she focus more on her schoolwork.

MORIKAMIS

PRESENTS

BMX BLITZ

A PRODUCTION OF

a Capstone company — publishers for children

written by **Scott Ciencin**
illustrated by **Aburtov**
inked by **Andres Esparza**
coloured by **Fares Maese**

designed and directed by **Bob Lentz**
edited by **Sean Tulien**
creative direction by **Heather Kindseth**
editorial management by **Donald Lemke**
editorial direction by **Michael Dahl**

Raintree is an imprint of Capstone Global Library, a company incorporated in England and Wales having its registered office at 264 Banbury Road, Oxford, OX2 7DY – Registered company number: 6695582

www.raintree.co.uk
myorders@raintree.co.uk

Text © Capstone Global Library Limited 2019
The moral rights of the proprietor have been asserted.

ISBN: 978 1 4747 7164 1
22 21 20 19 18
10 9 8 7 6 5 4 3 2 1

British Library Cataloguing in Publication Data
A full catalogue record for this book is available from the British Library.

Originated by Capstone Global Library Ltd
Printed and bound in India

I bet you're wondering what goes through your head when you're on live television.

The pressure *can* get to you.

But for me...

...it's nothing new.

My dad's a NASCAR racing champion. So, I'm used to being in the spotlight...

We're here live with BMX racer Luke Lawless and his father, famous NASCAR racing star Denny Lawless!

8

The country's best BMXers have flocked to the ultimate course.

The top three finishers get cash, trophies and an endorsement deal.

...But most of them will just go home with a couple of bruises.

CRUNCH!!

There's some stiff competition this year.

Houston Morakami is a two-time national BMX racing champ...

WHOOSH!

... and a competitive black belt with an attitude.

WHAM!

Peter Hildebrand is ruthless.

Heh.

Ah!

Watch it!

WHOOSH!

CLANK!

And he's always well prepared ...

But Peter's preparation won't matter in this race.

No one has even *seen* this course yet.

The BMX-BLITZ RACE COURSE is a multi-million-dollar track two years in the making.

Construction was under the tightest security.

CLICK!

... no matter what!

Download Complete

I had it won.

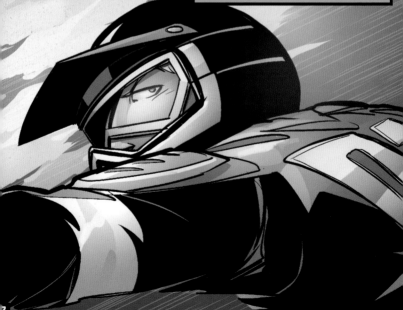

I was out in front of everybody, and . . .

But the expression on Pete's face told me everything I needed to know...

...cheaters never prosper.

RRIPP!

TWEEEEET!

Houston Morikami is the winner!

SPORTS ZONE
POSTGAME RECAP

BMX
BMX RACING

PNT
PAINTBALL

FBL
FOOTBALL

BSL
BASEBALL

BBL
BASKETBALL

HKY

HEATED RACE ENDS WITH SOLE GIRL CLAIMING GOLD!

BY THE NUMBERS

FINAL STANDINGS:

FIRST: H. MORIKAMI
SECOND: L. LAWLESS
THIRD: P. HILDEBRAND

STORY: Houston Morikami managed to fend off Luke Lawless and lay claim to first place. The two racers were neck and neck until the final sprint. Houston was able to pull ahead and take the lead – and she never looked back. When asked about how it felt to beat the boys in the BMX-Blitz, Houston said, "Whether you're a girl or a boy doesn't matter – I'm racing myself out there, anyway."

Sports Illustrated KIDS

UP NEXT: SI KIDS INFO CENTRE

BLZ vs BHS
3-1
TGR vs ROR
33-32
EAG vs BAN
14-7
SPA vs WLD
4-3
BAN vs ROR
21-15
RZR vs LIG
4-3
BLZ vs BHS
3-1

SZ POSTGAME EXTRA

WHERE *YOU* ANALYSE THE GAME!

BMX racing fans got a real treat today when Luke Lawless and Houston Morikami faced off against Peter Hildebrand in the BMX-Blitz! Let's go into the stands and ask some fans for their opinions on the day's events ...

DISCUSSION QUESTION 1

Peter stole blueprints for the BMX-Blitz race course, which gave him an unfair advantage. What kind of punishment should he receive?

DISCUSSION QUESTION 2

Houston and Luke become friends while competing against each other. Do you think opponents should also be friends? Why or why not?

WRITING PROMPT 1

Luke and Houston's parents don't always understand them. In what ways do your parents understand you? What kinds of things do they not understand? Write about it.

WRITING PROMPT 2

What is more important to you – winning or playing fair? Would you rather win and have no one cheer for you, or lose and have everyone on your side? Explain.

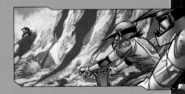

support or payment for sportspeople's expenses in exchange for advertising

travelled together in a group

paused uncertainly before acting

very strong

someone who is foolish or mean

be successful or thrive

met the standard needed to do something such as participate in a competition

cruel or without pity

last or final or best

SCOTT CIENCIN › Author

Scott Ciencin is a *New York Times* bestselling author of children's and adult fiction. He has written comic books, trading cards, video games and television shows, as well as many non-fiction projects. He lives in Florida, USA, with his beloved wife, Denise, and his best buddy, Bear, a golden retriever.

ABURTOV › Illustrator

Aburtov has worked in the comic book industry for more than 11 years. In that time, he has illustrated popular characters such as Wolverine, Iron Man, Blade and the Punisher. Recently, Aburtov started his own illustration studio called Graphikslava. He lives in Monterrey, Mexico, with his daughter, Ilka, and his beloved wife. Aburtov enjoys spending his spare time with family and friends.

ANDRES ESPARZA › Inker

Andres Esparza has been a graphic designer, colourist and illustrator for many different companies and agencies. Andres now works as a full-time artist for Graphikslava studio in Monterrey, Mexico. In his spare time, Andres loves to play basketball, hang out with family and friends, and listen to good music.

FARES MAESE › Colourist

Fares Maese is a graphic designer and illustrator. He has worked as a colourist for Marvel Comics, and as a concept artist for the card and role-playing games *Pathfinder* and *Warhammer*. Fares loves spending time playing video games with his Graphikslava colleagues, and he's an awesome drummer.

JAKE "SULLY" SULLIVAN IN:
TRACK TEAM TITANS

My friends weren't happy that I signed them up for track without asking first.

Get back here, Sully!

WHOOSH!

BARK! BARK!

We can't do track and field!

WHOOSH!

Actually, you guys just proved you *can!*

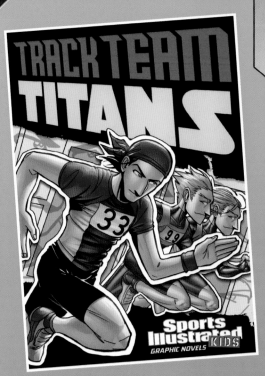
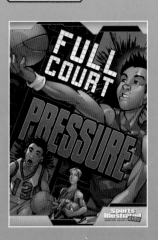

HOT SPORTS.
HOT
FORMAT!

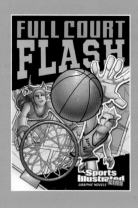

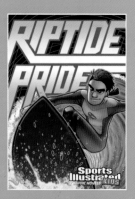

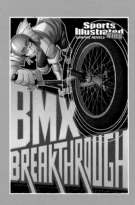